To Ellie, Henry, and Molly — A.C.
To Bennett and Sawyer — J.S.

Hey, need a squirrel for your book? I work for peanuts, but I prefer tacos.

This Is a ~~Squirrel~~ TACO!

By Andrew Cangelose

Illustrated by Josh Shipley

This is a squirrel.

Hi, my name is Taco, 'cause my favorite food is tacos! I'm really excited to be in this book! I can't wait to help you learn all about squirrels like me!

Squirrels are some of the cleanest rodents in the wild. They are known for having silky, soft fur.

Gotta give some credit to my prairie dog pal, Garbage. He's my stylist!
Hi, my name is Garbage, 'cause my favorite food is...
Save it for a prairie dog book. This book's about squirrels.

Squirrels love to eat nuts, acorns,
and even tree bark.

Tree bark??? I was told there'd be tacos. It's kind of the main reason I agreed to be in this book.

Squirrels can pack large amounts of food into their cheeks to transport back to their nests.

Squirrels can rotate their ankles completely
backward. This allows them to climb
in any direction.

Squirrels are great tree climbers
and love to jump from branch to branch.

I'm scared of heights!
I live in a bush!

Some squirrels, called flying squirrels, can glide through the air for distances of over 150 feet!

You've got the wrong squirrel!
My cousin Barry is the flyer
in the family!
AHHHHHHHHHH!!!!!!

Then they glide gently to the ground for a graceful landing.

The hawk is the natural predator of squirrels, swooping down from the air to swipe them right off the ground.

Whoa! Time out! This book needs fewer hawks and way more tacos. And when I say fewer hawks, I mean ZERO!

The hawk is th ator of squirrels, swoopi he air to swie th und.

The hawk is the ⬤ ▓▓▓ ator of
squirrels, swoop▓ ▓▓▓▓ he air to
swipe them ri▓ ▓▓▓▓ ▓und.

The ~~hawk~~ is the natural predator of squirrels, swooping do[wn] from [the a]i[r] to swipe them right off...

Boo

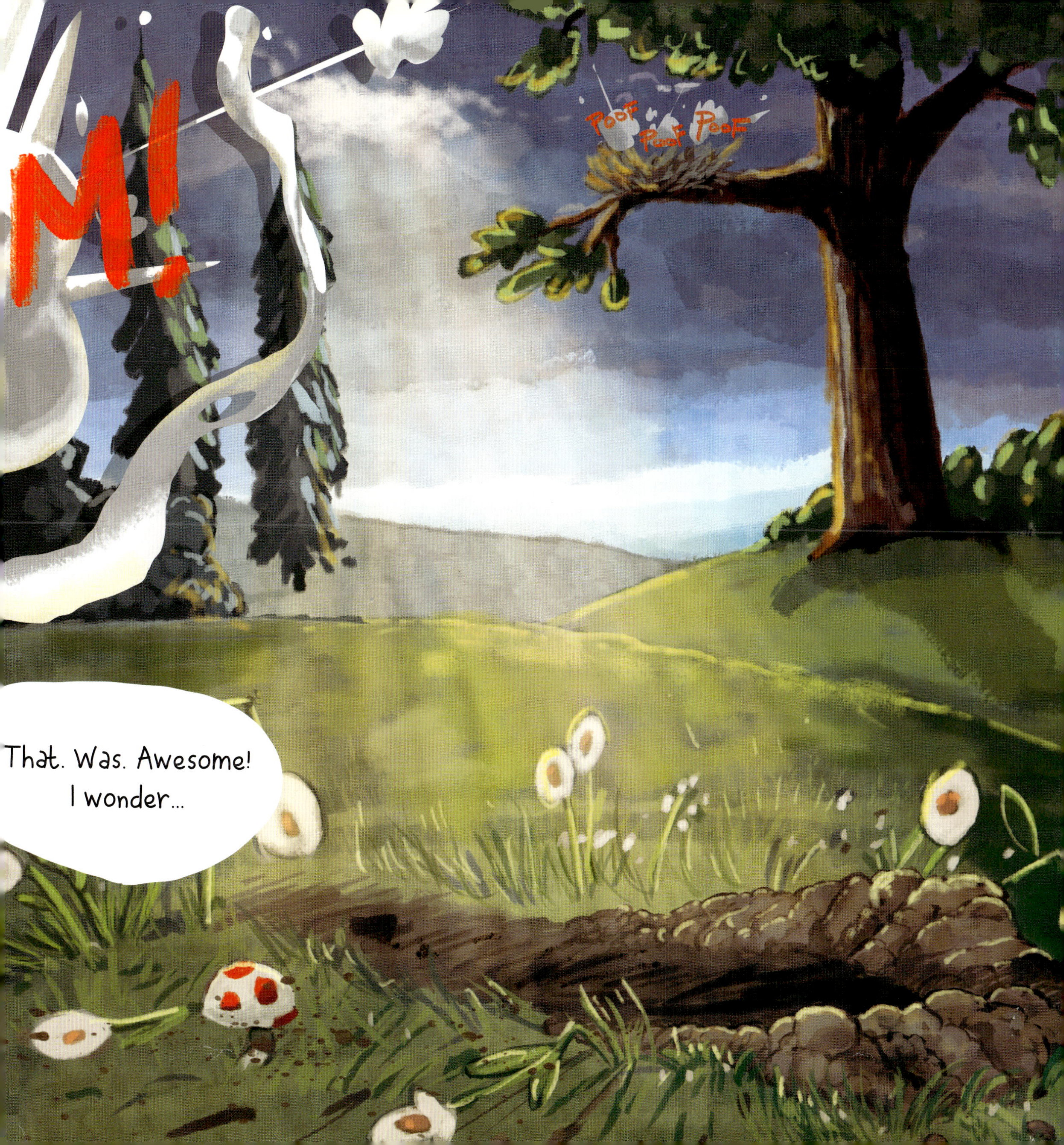
M!
POOF POOF POOF
That. Was. Awesome!
I wonder...

The ~~hawk~~ **TACO** is the natural predator of
TACOS ~~squirrels,~~ swooping down from the air to
swipe them right off the ground.

Now that's more like it!

TACO

The ~~hawk~~ is the natural predator of

TACOS

~~squirrels,~~ swooping down from the air to

swipe them right off the ground.

Taco hungry for tacos! Swoop time!
Who invited this guy? Hey, salsa breath! You're in the wrong book!

The ~~hawk~~ **Taco** is the natural predator of ~~squirrels~~ **Tacos**, swooping down from the air to swipe them right off the ground.

A giant taco—sheesh! He's lucky I have a rule about eating things with faces.

Taco, the squirrel
(and not an actual giant, talking taco),
is the natural predator
of tacos.

Squirrels are great eaters
and can eat their body weight in
tacos ~~food~~ in just a ~~week.~~ day.

Kids, remember: If you want tacos in your story, then YOU make sure there are tacos in your story.

ISBN: 978-1-941302-72-9

Library of Congress Control Number: 2017963044

www.lionforge.com